# Prince Cinders
## by
## Babette Cole

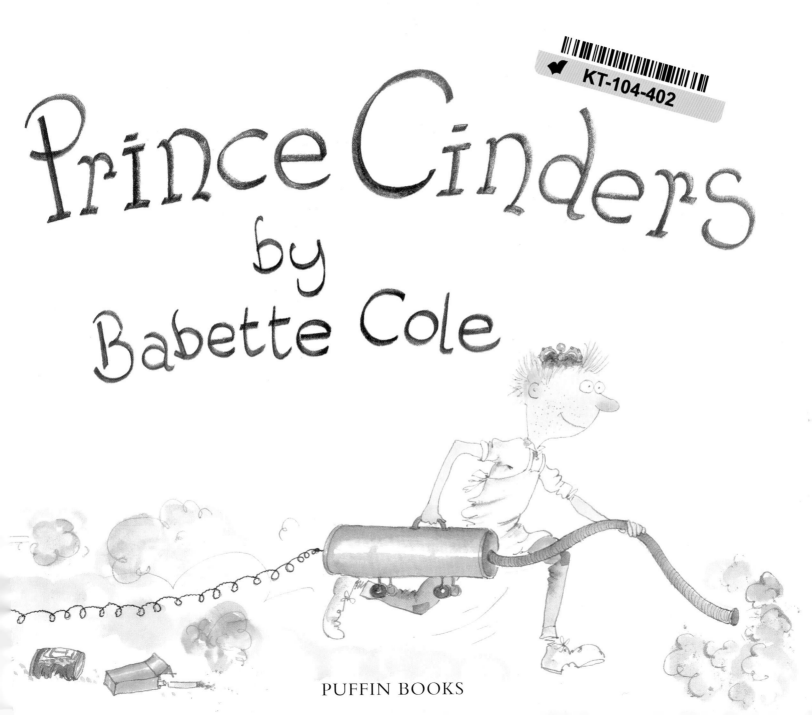

PUFFIN BOOKS

Prince Cinders was not much of a prince.
He was small, spotty, scruffy and skinny.

He had three big hairy brothers who were
always teasing him about his looks.

They spent their time going to the Palace Disco
with princess girlfriends.

They made poor Prince Cinders stay behind and clean up after them.

When his work was done he would sit by the fire
and wish he was big and hairy like his brothers.

One Saturday night, when he was washing the socks, a dirty fairy fell down the chimney.

"All your wishes shall be granted,"
cried the fairy.
"Ziz Ziz Boom, Tic Tac Ta,
This empty can shall be a car."

"Bif Bang Bong, Bo Bo Bo, to the disco you shall go!"

"That can't be right!" said the fairy.

"Toe of rat and eye of newt,
your rags will turn into a suit!"

("Crumbs," thought the fairy,
"I didn't mean a SWIM suit!"

"Your greatest wish I'll grant to you. You SHALL be big
and hairy too!"

Prince Cinders got
big and hairy
all right!

"Rats!" said the fairy.
"Wrong again, but I'm sure
it all wears off at midnight."

Prince Cinders didn't know he was a big hairy
monkey because that's
the kind of spell
it was.

He thought he looked pretty good!

So off he went to the disco. The car was too
small to drive but he made the best of it.

But when he arrived at the Royal Rave up,

he was too big to fit through the door!

He decided to take the bus home.
A pretty princess was waiting at the stop.

"When's the next bus?" he grunted.

Luckily, midnight struck and Prince Cinders changed back into himself.

The princess thought he had saved her by frightening away the big hairy monkey!

"Wait!" she shouted, but Prince Cinders was
too shy. He even lost his trousers in the rush!

The princess was none other than the rich and beautiful Princess Lovelypenny. She put out a proclamation to find the owner of the trousers.

Every prince for miles around tried to force the trousers on.

But they wriggled about and refused to fit any of them!

Of course Prince Cinders' brothers all fought
to get into the trousers at once . . .

"Let him try,"
commanded the
princess, pointing
at Cinders.

"They won't fit that little squirt," sneered his brothers.

. . . But they did!
Princess Lovelypenny proposed immediately.

So Prince Cinders married Princess Lovelypenny and lived in luxury, happily ever after . . .

And Princess Lovelypenny had a word with the
fairy about his big hairy brothers . . .

. . . whom she turned into house fairies.
And they flitted around the palace doing the housework
for ever and ever.